W9-CXT-955

A Whitman TWEEN-AGE Book

In-between books for in-between readers.

IT'S A MYSTERY!

Stories of Suspense

ABOUT THIS BOOK

Eerie music coming from a woods late at night near Mark's and Billy's camp . . .

An electric train which runs by itself—or so it seems to Dave . . .

A lonely tower—it seems like a good place to explore, until Diane and Peg find themselves watching a secret message being flashed across the river . . .

A strange object in a clearing which looks to Tom and Andy like something from outer space . . .

Thumping and scratching noises at Becky and Ray's door on a blustery winter evening . . .

Whether or not you can guess the answers to all these mysterious happenings, you will find spine-tingling fun and many new friends in IT'S A MYSTERY!

IT'S A MYSTERY!

Stories of Suspense

by Mildred Bingham

Illustrated by Wendell Kling and Al Stine

Whitman Publishing Company • Racine, Wisconsin

Library of Congress Catalog Card Number 65-23326

WHITMAN PUBLISHING COMPANY
RACINE, WISCONSIN
Printed in the U.S.A. by Western Printing and Lithographing Company

CONTENTS

MYSTERY IN THE TRAIN ROOM

Danny had not thought much about his electric train for a long time. The clear *Honk! Honk!* of a diesel engine somewhere far away this cool night reminded him of Old Casey.

He pushed his head deeper into his pillow. "Maybe," he thought, "I'll go down and give that old engine a few turns around the track . . . tomorrow.

Dad said he was going to sell it . . . if I didn't start showing more interest in it. He wouldn't really sell it, I'll bet. Why, he's had Old Casey since he was a little boy. But . . . he sounded like he meant it. Maybe I'll. . . ." Danny fell asleep.

He did not give another thought to Old Casey until almost bedtime the next night. Then his father asked him to see if the basement lights were still on.

"Sure, Dad," said Danny. "And I think I'll take a quick look at Old Casey."

"Well," his father said with a surprised look. "Fine, son!"

Danny felt good that he had surprised and pleased his father. He bounced happily down the steps. The train room was dark. He reached into the blackness, feeling for the light switch.

Suddenly a dim red light glowed through the darkness. Something hummed, buzzed softly. The red light flickered off, then on again.

"The transformer's on!" cried Danny. He flipped the light switch and hurried to the train table. "No!" he gasped. "What happened?"

Old Casey was puffing smoke but not moving.

Two flatcars were across the track. A passenger car leaned against the caboose. Trees were knocked over.

"Who plugged in the transformer? And who turned on my train?" frowned Danny. He jerked the cord from the electric outlet on the wall. "Must have been some little kids visiting Mom with their mother," he decided. He checked the wiring from the transformer to the tracks. "Looks okay. Wonder how long it's been this way?"

Carefully he set each tree, each car in its proper place.

"Wonder why the transformer turned on? Maybe something's wrong with the wiring," he said to himself.

"Anything wrong down there, Danny?" his father called.

"Somebody plugged in the train!" yelled Danny.

"Well, the circuit breaker ought to have saved that old transformer," said his father. "But don't try it now, son. I'll look at it later tonight."

"Okay, Dad!" shouted Danny. He smiled down at each dusty building, each piece of his train village. His father had made most of them. The town looked like one in the old West. "Dad and I used to have fun around this table," he remembered. "Hope he does check the wiring tonight. It'll be fun to be an engineer again. But I'll tell Mom to keep little kids away from my train!" And he went back upstairs.

The next morning at breakfast his mother said, "I'm sorry, Danny. I was showing Mrs. Jordan's boys the old train. She wants to buy one soon. And I forgot to pull the cord when they left."

And his father said happily, "The old transformer wasn't burned out, thanks to the circuit breaker box."

"Swell!" smiled Danny. "I'll go down for a quick look. If everything's still working, maybe Bill will come over after school." He hurried downstairs.

But when he reached the doorway to the train room, something *was* wrong. Old Casey and all the cars were racing around the track again.

"Dad!" Danny yelled upward.

"Yes?" answered his father from the top of the stairs. "Works pretty well, huh, son? Couldn't get Old Casey's whistle to blow, though. Transformer's On and Off buttons are still loose. Maybe I'll get a new one."

"But didn't you unplug the cord?" asked Danny.

"Hmmm. Come to think of it, I forgot to, son," said his father. "Sorry. Talk to you later. I'm late for work."

Danny stared down at the busy train. "He left it plugged in. But Dad wouldn't have left Old Casey *running,"* thought Danny. "Maybe it's the loose buttons on the transformer, or maybe it's the wiring. Maybe we have ghosts down here!"

He glanced around the room. Stacks of boxes, old boards, and magazines leaned against the walls. Shelves were filled with dusty, cobwebby things. "Sure is a mess," he told himself. "And gloomy. And kind of spooky!"

OOOOEEE! OOOOEEEEEE!

Danny jumped, frightened. Old Casey's whistle had started working again!

"Well, something's causing a lot of mysterious things to happen down here," he said. "If it isn't the transformer, or the wiring, maybe there *is* a ghost!" He shivered at the thought and poked the Off button. Then he darted up the stairs.

Danny thought about his train a lot during school that day. He knew he had turned the transformer off. But he worried about leaving it plugged in. He had never done that before. He wondered about ghosts. He had never seen one, but. . . .

After school he ran all the way home in a rainstorm. "I'm not going in that room until Bill comes over!" he kept thinking.

He waited for Bill on the bottom basement step. He could see into the gloomy train room. Old

DRY GULCH
HOTEL
LIVERY

Casey was quiet, or at least Danny thought he was. The rumbling thunder had not stopped.

Suddenly, OOOOEEEE!

Danny trembled. "Is it Old Casey this time or a —a ghost?" he worried. Slowly he stood up and crept close to the doorway. He wanted one quick look at whatever was in there. He pressed his stomach against the wall. Carefully, he peeked into the room.

All was quiet, almost dark. Cloudy daylight from the small high window above the train table made everything look spooky. Icy goose bumps rippled down Danny's back. He jerked his head out of the room. He wanted to run. But Bill was coming.

A door banged upstairs. "He's in the basement with his train, Bill," Danny heard his mother say.

Danny moved stiffly back to the train room doorway. The red light was on again. Old Casey was moving on the track!

"I've got to go in there!" he told himself. "I don't want Bill to think I'm chicken, not if it's only the wiring." He heard Bill's footsteps above him.

A feeling of new courage flashed through Danny. Quickly he reached for the light switch. The bright light showed nothing but the busy train. He ran to the table and saw the church steeple swaying. The station house next to the transformer rattled. Danny froze to the spot, fearing what might happen next.

"Danny?" It was Bill in the train room doorway. "Sun's coming out. Let's go outside. Who wants to play with trains?"

"Sshh," was all Danny could say.

"Hey! Look at that!" gulped Bill behind Danny. "The church fell over!"

Danny saw a small gray thing dart across the table. "It went into the tunnel," he said excitedly. "I think it's a mouse! Bet there's another in the station house."

Bill started to lift the station house.

"Wait!" cried Danny. "I want to see something!" He ran to the light switch and darkened the room.

"I didn't know you had an old-fashioned train," Bill said softly. "This is really something, just like the old West!"

"Sshh," whispered Danny, pulling Bill away from the table. "I want to see if mice, or whatever they are, can turn the transformer on and off."

LIVERY
HOTEL
HOTEL

"They might've chewed wires," said Bill, "but—"

"Well, it's either mice or chipmunks—or some kind of ghost!" Danny told him.

Bill said no more.

They stared at the dark tunnel, then at the station house. Bright sunshine from the high window fell across part of the table.

"Look!" cried Danny.

A small gray thing darted out of the tunnel. It

ran down the track and hid in the toppled church.

"It's just a mouse!" sighed Bill. "And there's another peeking out of the station house!"

Danny looked in time to see a mouse crawling out a station house window. Its front feet touched down on the loose transformer button. The red light flashed on. Old Casey moved cars forward. And the mouse vanished through the window of the Dry Gulch Hotel.

"Just mice!" laughed Danny. He lifted the roof of the station house. "Look, they're making a nest!"

"Hope they didn't hurt anything," said Bill. He tapped the Off button. "Hey, you need a new transformer. I have a pretty powerful one I don't use, Danny, with a built-in circuit breaker."

"Yep, that one's got to go," agreed Danny.

"I'll go get mine! And we could clean up everything." Bill was halfway up the stairs before he added, "Be back in a jiff, chief engineer!"

Danny pulled the electric cord from the wall outlet. He felt sure about things for the first time all day. He knew he wouldn't forget Old Casey and the mystery in the train room for a long, long time.

THE BOX

Meg and her little brother Jimmy thought Gracie was the best big dog in the world. Except when Gracie borrowed things from neighbors. Meg and Jimmy had to return everything Gracie borrowed.

Today they had given Mr. Price his fishing boot. They put back Mrs. Sadler's porch cushion. They gave Jeff Jordan his leaky basketball. And, they still had one more thing to return to someone. A flat, wooden box.

It wasn't a big box. It was about the size of a thick library book. The wood was dark and scratched. And the box was locked.

Meg and Jimmy—and Gracie—had stopped at every house where Gracie usually borrowed things. But the locked box didn't belong to any neighbor.

"We'll just have to try another street and ask strangers," sighed Meg.

They walked—with Gracie—down the sidewalk toward the next street.

"Wish we could open it," said Jimmy. He shook the box. Things inside rattled and clinked. "If we knew what was inside we could find the owner quicker."

"Let Gracie smell it," said Meg. "Maybe she'll show us where she got it."

Jimmy stuck the box under Gracie's long nose. "Show us, Gracie!"

Gracie sniffed the box. Then she grabbed it and ran down the sidewalk.

Meg and Jimmy ran after her.

"She's going down Lookout Street!" panted Meg. "Good girl, Gracie!"

Suddenly Gracie stopped in front of the house on the corner. She turned around, wagged her tail, and dropped the box. It banged loudly on the sidewalk.

"Gracie!" scolded Meg. "Did you break it?"

Gracie darted around the house on the corner.

Meg and Jimmy raced toward the box. They could see white and shiny things scattered on the sidewalk.

"You shouldn't have scolded her!" said Jimmy. "Now we don't know which house to stop at!"

"But she thought I wanted to play," explained Meg. "Look, Jimmy! Little knives!" She stopped to pick up a knife. The blade of the small knife was curved into a hook. "I've never seen one like this!"

"And the handles look like bones!" added Jimmy.

"Oooeee!" squealed Meg. "Who would want them?"

Jimmy laughed. "Gracie wanted the bones!"

Meg laughed, too. But she was careful as she placed the hooked knife and a curved knife and a saw-toothed knife into the box. Jimmy dropped in three triangle-shaped knives.

"Now," said Meg, "we know what's inside the

box. But who would use all these knives?"

"A doctor, maybe!" Jimmy grabbed up the box. "Just like I'm going to be when I get big!"

"Then," smiled Meg, "let's see if a doctor lives here." She hurried up the walk to the house on the corner.

"Hey!" Jimmy yelled from the sidewalk. "I know somebody who lives on this street. Jeff says a witch lives here. He saw her once and—"

"Be quiet, Jimmy. Someone will hear you," Meg scolded from the porch steps. "You don't have to come with me—if you're afraid."

"Aw, who's afraid!" Jimmy ran up the steps with Meg.

Meg knocked gently on the front door.

"I wish Gracie would come back to us," Jimmy said softly.

"Don't be such a scaredy-cat," teased Meg. She knocked on the door again.

"Well, Jeff said he saw some scary faces looking out a big back window," Jimmy chattered. "And this lady was stirring some awful looking stuff in an old tub in her backyard and—"

"Stop worrying about witches, Jimmy," Meg said, frowning down at him.

They waited quietly for the door to open. Nothing happened.

"Come on, Meg," begged Jimmy. "Let's try another house."

"Wait!" The door opened slowly, only an inch or two.

"I don't want any flower seeds or magazines," said a woman.

"But we have a box," Meg explained. "We're trying to find its owner."

The door opened a little more.

"Oh?" said the woman. "What kind of box?"

Jimmy pushed the box into Meg's hands.

"That's mine. I'm sure," smiled the woman. She reached out for the box. Her hand was smeared with gluey-looking brown stuff.

Meg dropped the box into the hand. "We're so glad we finally found its owner."

The woman opened the door wider. She lifted the box lid and seemed to be counting the strange-shaped knives.

Just then Meg saw the woman's apron. It was spotted with more of the gluey-looking brown stuff. Meg looked at Jimmy. He was staring at the apron, too.

"We have to go, Meg!" gulped Jimmy. He started down the porch steps.

"Well, bye," Meg said to the woman.

"Wait!" called the woman. "You deserve a reward for returning my box to me. These are my favorite tools."

"We don't want a reward!" Jimmy said quickly. "That's not why we brought it back."

"Oh, but I insist," smiled the woman. She stood away from the doorway. "Won't you come in? Just for a minute, please?"

Meg gave Jimmy a quick "Let's do!" look and walked into the hallway.

Jimmy followed her, saying, "We can wait here, Meg. Just for a minute."

The woman closed the door. "I'll hurry," she said and walked down the dimly lit hallway.

"She's not a doctor!" Jimmy whispered. "With

all that stuff all over her! Jeff was right."

"Oh, Jimmy," sighed Meg. "You shouldn't believe everything Jeff says. It's probably just paint."

"Then what does she do with those little knives we found?" worried Jimmy.

Suddenly the woman called from the end of the hallway. "Won't you come back here? It's a much cheerier place for some cookies."

"Sure," smiled Meg. Without a glance at Jimmy, she walked down the hall.

"We have to hurry, Meg, remember?" Jimmy said loudly. But he followed her.

"I'll not keep you," said the woman. "But I do have a dog's head you children might like to see."

Quickly Jimmy bumped Meg and whispered, "I told you. I'm not going to look at it!"

Suddenly Meg's stomach felt funny. She didn't want to see a dog's head, either. Not a real one.

"Maybe," she thought, "it's just a painting. But what would the woman do with those strange little knives?"

Just then the woman opened a door. They walked into a big, bright kitchen.

"I'll clean my hands," said the woman taking off her apron, "and see that you get something special." She hurried into another room.

Meg began to relax in the cheerful kitchen. "See how nice she is?" she asked Jimmy.

But Jimmy was staring at a long table. "Look, Meg!" he whispered excitedly.

Meg moved closer to the table. A big blob of gluey-looking brown stuff was in the center of the tabletop.

"That's not like paint!" Jimmy said from behind her.

"Sshh," whispered Meg. "She's coming!"

"Children," called the woman from the other room, "come and see this."

"The dog's head!" gulped Jimmy.

Again Meg hoped it was only a painting, a pretty picture of a brown dog's head. Slowly she walked toward the other room. She felt Jimmy holding onto her sweater. And he stayed behind her.

"It's just right to take out now," said the woman as they walked into the room. She was staring into a big metal box. "Come and see her beautiful head."

Meg took two more steps and saw a small window in the front of the box. And on a shelf inside was a red-brown dog's head! "It's Gracie!" cried Meg.

"Gracie?" gulped Jimmy. He hugged Meg and looked through the small window. "What did you do to our dog?" He began to cry. "Poor Gracie!"

Suddenly a loud "Woof!" came from behind them! They turned and saw Gracie flopping her tail.

"But, but—" cried Jimmy, looking first at Gracie, then at the dog's head.

"Children!" The woman looked surprised. "What did you think was in my kiln?"

"I knew what it was!" laughed Meg.

"But it looks real," Jimmy grinned shyly.

"Thank you," smiled the woman. "I'm a sculptor, children. I carved the dog's head from brown clay. It turns red-brown—just like your Gracie—when it's baked." She rubbed Gracie's head and added, "She's been coming to visit me every day. And I leave the door open for her. She stays long enough for me to study her big, beautiful Irish setter head."

"That's how Gracie got your box!" sighed Meg.

"Oh, that reminds me," said the woman. "A reward for my box." She seemed to be thinking, then continued, "You shall have Gracie's head, if you want it!"

"Okay, Jimmy?" Meg asked excitedly.

"Oh, boy, yes!" agreed Jimmy.

And while they—and Gracie—nibbled cookies around the long table, the woman explained how she mixed brown clay in an old tub. And she showed them how she carved heads from the clay with little knives, the ones from the box Gracie had borrowed.

THE TRIP

"When will we be out of these hills, Dad?" Dave asked sleepily from the backseat.

"In a few more miles," answered his father. "Traffic's heavy on the curves."

Dave flipped a pencil against his bingo card. "I'll never find a greenhouse or a rooster on a roof—or anything interesting in these hills," he sighed.

"Dave"—his mother smiled back at him—"want to play 'Let's take a trip' for a while?"

"Aw, Mom," said Dave. "That's for little kids like Martha. And she'll sleep for hours."

"Oh, I'll bet something interesting will pass us once in a while," coaxed his mother.

"Okay," agreed Dave. "Front starts."

"I'm taking a trip," began his mother, "and I'll be driving a—a—"

Dave looked at the road ahead. It was straighter now. A car could pass them. He looked at the road behind them. "Here comes one, Mom! Wait'll you see it! It's a—a—"

"A bread truck!" laughed his mother. "Let's see what your father will be driving."

"Take my turn, Dave," said his father. "I want to watch these curves."

Dave looked at the road behind them. "Don't pass yet, Dad. My trip car's coming fast. It's going to pass us. Aw, it's a truck!" He watched the white truck speeding closer. "Looks like the one you have at the store, Dad," He sat back in his seat. "That's no fun to take a trip in," he sighed.

Then he looked out just as his trip truck zoomed past his window. "Dad! It *was* your truck!" he cried. "It said 'Springfield Hardware' on the door! In blue letters!"

"We don't deliver this close to Johnstown, Dave," said his father. "Are you sure it said *Hardware?*"

"I sure am!" answered Dave. "What's it doing up here?"

"Hmm," muttered his father. "We don't have any business with stores up here, but—"

"What if somebody stole the truck!" interrupted Dave. "Or maybe somebody at the store is trying to catch up with us!"

"We've been driving less than an hour," his mother added quickly.

"Well, we'd better find out! Keep your eyes on

the truck, Dave," said his father. "I'll try to catch it before we get into Johnstown traffic. We're almost there."

Dave pressed his cheek against the window. He couldn't see the white truck. The bread truck was too tall. But there was a left curve in the road ahead. He breathed excitedly. Never before had they been hunted on the highway. Or, he thought with a shiver, they might be on the trail of a truck robber!

He watched the white truck move around the left curve. It was still going fast. So was the bread truck. And then the white truck disappeared around a high hill!

When their car curved around the hill, Dave saw no white truck. Only the beginning of Johnstown was beyond the bread truck. He sat tall and stiff with excitement. He would have to check every white truck in the town traffic!

They moved slowly. Three blocks. Four blocks. Dave knew Johnstown's main street wasn't much longer. There were no white delivery trucks in town.

Suddenly his father said, "Dave! Look there, behind us!"

DWARE
CARRISON

Dave turned to look through the back window. A white truck was following close behind them now!

"If it's ours," said his father, "the driver must've made a wrong turn."

"I can't tell if it's the same one, Dad," said Dave. "It'll have to pass us so I can see the name on the door."

"Do you recognize the driver, Dave?" his mother asked.

Dave studied the driver's face. "No, Mom. He's not close enough. And he's wearing dark glasses and a hat."

Dave wondered if he was watching a friend. *I'll find out!* he said to himself. He stuck his nose close to the back window. He waved both hands at the man in the white truck. "Hope he recognizes *me!*" he said loudly.

But the driver didn't smile or wave back.

"He doesn't know me, Dad!" cried Dave.

"He might not be able to see you," said his father. "The sun's reflecting on car windows ahead of me."

Dave wished he had something for a signal. "The bingo card!" he remembered. He grabbed Martha's box of crayons, flipped the card over, and printed the word S T O P! He rolled down his window and waved the sign at the driver.

This time Dave could see white teeth smiling back at him. "I think he thinks I'm just teasing!" worried Dave.

"Sit back, son! I can pass, now," said his father. "I'll try to stop it up ahead."

Dave dropped down in his seat. Their car spurted past the bread truck. Up the road was a wide driveway. Dave knew his father was going to stop there. And his father was going to signal the white truck to stop!

"If a stranger gets out of that truck . . ." Dave worried.

He looked quickly at the building at the end of the wide driveway. It was a restaurant. He could run in there for help if his father needed it. He looked back at the white truck. He almost wished it wouldn't stop.

"No one is to get out of this car!" ordered his

STOP

father. He parked their car and jumped out.

Dave watched him hurry to the edge of the road. As soon as the bread truck roared past them, his father waved both hands at the white truck. "Would a robber stop?" Dave wondered. The truck was slowing down. He hoped his father knew the driver.

The white truck stopped not far behind their car. The truck door opened. *"Springfield Hardware!"* read Dave. "The driver's getting out, Mom!"

"It looks like Mr. Martin, from the store!" his mother said happily.

"It is!" cried Dave. "Here they come! Hi, Mr. Martin!" he yelled. "Didn't you know me back there? I waved to you."

"I thought that boy looked like you, Dave," said Mr. Martin. "But my mind was busy thinking about finding a light blue car with a family of *four* in it. I didn't see Martha and couldn't see your father's face. And, with my sunglasses on, your car looked green."

"But why were you hunting us?" asked Dave.

"Your Dad is driving without his driver's license," explained Mr. Martin. "And that's against the law."

"I left it in the key case for the truck, Dave," said his father. He hurried to their car. "Sit down, son. We have to find your mother's bread truck. A friend of Mr. Martin's is driving it, trying to find us. We have to let him know I have the license."

"He knows the roads up this way better than I do," added Mr. Martin. "And he thinks you'll be in Brownsville for lunch. Be sure Martha sits up. And remember, he's wearing dark glasses, too. Have a good trip!" he called as their car moved back onto the road.

"Bye!" waved Dave.

"Bye!" Martha was awake and waving, too. "Look, Dave! There's another bingo!" she said.

Dave saw the rooster on top of the restaurant behind them. He marked his bingo card. Then he turned it over. He might need that S T O P! again. He rolled up his window and pressed his cheek against it. Now, he had to watch for a bread truck. "What a trip!" he sighed excitedly.

* * *

P. S. Yes, they caught up with the bread truck before Brownsville. It had stopped at a service station next to a garden store with a greenhouse behind it.

LOST BALL

Mary stomped past the pitcher's mound and headed for right field. "I was supposed to be short-stop after supper!" she grumbled to herself. "Just because I'm a girl I have to play where they say. Nothing exciting happens back here. Most of the batters don't hit this way. Or even this far. Except for Dave."

"Hey, Mary! Your big fat cat is on the field again!" yelled Sam in center field. "And move back more!"

"All right!" Mary called grumpily. She turned around. "Stop following me, Alice-Cat!" She stomped her foot. "Go home!" Her big cat only waddled slowly toward the edge of the diamond.

"Be ready for a hard hit, Mary," Sam yelled again. "And we might need a long, hard throw to third base."

Mary squinted toward home plate. Dave was swinging a bat. Quickly she backed to the end of the ball field and glanced down at the tall weeds at the bottom of the hill. "If I miss!" she thought.

"Strike one!" Sam echoed the umpire.

Mary fidgeted, waiting for the next pitch. She hoped Dave got this one long hit. She wanted to show them a good catch and a long hard throw from right field.

The next throw from the pitcher cracked against Dave's bat. The ball sailed high toward right field.

"It's yours, Mary!" shouted Sam. "Watch it! Watch it!"

Her glove was ready, waiting for the catch. The ball fell fast. Mary leaped high for it. But she didn't leap high enough!

"Aw, a home run!" she heard Sam yell as she looked down the hill. She saw the ball resting against a rock halfway down the slope. She scooted toward it. When she was almost to the ball, her shoe loosened a rock. The rock rolled down to the ball. The ball bounced down the hill.

Oh, Mary! she scolded herself. *Now they probably won't let you finish the game!*

"Hey, Mary! Want some help?" Sam called from the top of the hill.

"The ball's in the weeds," she answered.

"Lost ball! Come on!" Sam yelled to the other players.

Mary slid farther down the hill. Then she jumped from a big rock above the spring trickling water into the brook. She landed in weeds at the edge of the water.

"Yahoo!" yelled the others, sliding down the hill after her.

Mary didn't look up. She wanted to find the ball

before the others flattened the weeds. But—she had a sudden thought—what if it had landed in the brook. She hadn't seen it go into the weeds!

She hurried to the brook. There, on the other side of the rock-filled water, she saw the ball. It was bobbing safely between two large rocks and the weedy bank.

"I found it!" she shouted happily. "Go on back! It's in the water! I can get it!" She yanked off her shoes.

"Yea for Mary!" shouted the others. And they scrambled back up the hill.

Mary watched them for only a moment while she pulled off her socks. But when she looked back at the ball, it was gone.

"It must have floated downstream!" she told herself. She hurried along the bank. Her eyes searched around every rock sticking out of the water.

"Come on, Mary," called Sam from the hilltop.

"I lost it again!" Mary told him.

"I'll tell the fellas," Sam sighed loudly.

"No," yelled Mary. "Come and help me catch it!" She moved slowly along the bank of the brook.

"The current's not fast," she said to herself. "How could the ball get this far down, with so many rocks in the water?"

"See it yet?" Sam asked, running up behind her.

Mary shook her head. "I can't figure out how it got away from those two big rocks near the weeds. You watch this side. I'll keep my eyes on the other bank. Maybe it's stuck again."

"I hope so," said Sam. "It's going to get dark soon."

Suddenly Mary saw the ball roll out of the weeds and plop into the water. "Look, Sam!" She pointed to the ball bobbing against a big rock near the weeds on the other side of the brook.

"I saw it fall in!" said Sam. "Get it! Before it floats away!"

Mary stepped into the water. And then she saw the weeds flutter above the ball. Quickly she stepped back to the bank. "Something's over there, Sam!"

"Uh-huh." Sam was staring at the weeds, too. "And that ball just didn't roll out by itself!"

"Maybe one of the little kids is playing a trick on us," said Mary.

"Look! The weeds are moving again!" cried Sam.

"Oh, stop teasing, whoever you are," Mary called. "We want to finish the game."

But not a giggle, not a sound, came from the weeds. Not even a flutter.

"Alice-Cat?" called Mary. "Are you hiding over there?"

"You and that cat!" said Sam. "Here, big fat Alice-Cat!"

They watched the weeds. Nothing moved.

"Well," said Sam. "Are you afraid to wade over and get the ball?"

"No, but—" Mary didn't take her eyes away from the weeds. "But, Sam, whatever rolled the ball into the water could've taken it back where I first found it. Let's wait just a minute. Maybe we can see what did it. Just in case somebody misses another ball and—"

"Okay," agreed Sam. "But *just* a minute."

They stared at the ball and the weeds. Slowly five clawed fingerlike toes reached out. They curved, then batted at the ball.

"Boy! What's that?" whispered Mary.

"Not your cat!" answered Sam.

Splash! The clawed paw flipped the ball out of the water into the weeds.

"Aw, Mary," said Sam. "We shouldn't have waited. Now it's lost."

The weeds rustled, then parted. Two bright eyes in a dark furry face looked straight at them.

"A raccoon!" laughed Mary. "He was washing our ball for his supper, I'll bet! He probably thinks it's a big nut."

"Won't he be surprised when he bites into it!" laughed Sam. "Look at him. Just sitting there, holding the ball. He's not even afraid of us."

"City coons are used to people," Mary told him. "But I'm not going after that ball!"

"Let's call the others!" Sam said quickly. "All of us could get it away from him!"

"But he might run away with it before they got down here," reasoned Mary. "Wish we had a stick to poke him with."

Suddenly something rubbed against Mary's leg. "Alice-Cat!" she cried and grabbed up her cat. "She's not afraid of anything, Sam! And she's as big as he is!" She tossed the cat across the brook. "Just tease him a little, girl," coaxed Mary. "Make him drop the ball."

"Get him, big fat Alice-Cat!" Sam said excitedly.

"Stop calling her that!" Mary said angrily. "It sounds mean! She might save the ball!"

"I'm sorry, Mary," Sam said softly.

They could hear the big cat hissing in the weeds. The raccoon was growling in her direction. But he still held onto the ball.

REEEOWORH! snarled the cat.

"She's almost to him!" worried Mary.

"Look at his mean teeth!" said Sam.

REEOWORH!

The raccoon wrinkled its nose and snarled back. And he dropped the ball.

"Get it!" cried Sam. "Before it floats away!"

"Not with that coon there!" Mary told him.

All at once the raccoon sank back into the weeds.

"He'll hurt Alice!" cried Mary. "I wish I hadn't

thrown her over there! Just to get an old ball! Come back, Alice."

"Hold it, Mary!" said Sam. "Listen."

The snarling and hissing had stopped.

"Oh," sighed Mary. "They didn't fight."

"Didn't you know," said Sam, "that raccoons will run for a tree before they'll fight? I'll bet Alice-Cat knew that. She showed him who was boss."

"Here, girl!" Mary called happily. And she splashed into the brook.

Meeow! Alice-Cat poked her head out of the weeds.

Mary picked her up, scooped up the ball, and waded back to Sam.

"Say, Mary," said Sam. "If I can talk the fellas into letting you play shortstop again, will you let Alice-Cat be our team mascot? We might need her to chase away that coon again."

"It's all right with me," said Mary. "About her being a mascot, I mean. But I'll stay in right field. I need to practice jumping for high hits. And Dave might get to bat again before dark," she added with a grin. "Come on! Let's play ball!"

WHEN THE SLEIGH BELLS JINGLED

"Hey, Georgie," Tim called to his brother. "Tell Mr. Bodi to wait for me if the bus comes early!" He zipped up his warm coat and ran out into the cold, sunny morning.

He ran as fast as he could in the deep, dry snow. "Boy, am I glad we're the last ones to get on the school bus," he thought. "It's light enough now to see if the middle of the pond's frozen. And it sure should be after last night."

He climbed up a glistening snowdrift. He slid down it, smiling. He could see white ice on the pond in the pasture. "Look's like we play hockey today!" he said excitedly. "If the middle's not mushy."

He ran toward the pond at the foot of a low hill. A thin ribbon of smoke curling above it and the green tops of the spruce woods reminded him of Mr. Hanson.

"He said he'd start cutting Christmas trees for the supermarket any day," Tim remembered. "This year I get to help him."

He stepped carefully onto the white ice at the edge of the pond. Slowly he slid toward the middle.

Suddenly he saw shadowed marks in a patch of snow ahead of him. "If that's mushy . . ." he worried.

He inched his way closer. The ice didn't crack. And the shadowed marks were dry.

"Just deer tracks," he sighed. "And big ones, too. Wonder if it was that old buck Mr. Hanson's always trying to protect from hunters."

He followed a few more of the two-toed hoof-prints. All at once he realized he had passed the middle of the pond. "If it was that buck, the ice *has* to be safe for hockey! He weighs hundreds of pounds. Boy, wait'll I tell the boys on the bus!" he said and turned toward home.

But just then he heard sleigh bells jingling from the other side of the low hill. "Hey! Mr. Hanson didn't say he was going to start cutting trees today." He listened to the jingling. "Sure sounds like he's got the bell harness on the horses. And if he needs me after school, I can't play hockey. I'd better find out now, before the bus comes."

He slid across the white ice and scrambled up the slippery hill. When he looked down, the old tree sled was sitting where it always did in the barnyard. "He's still in the barn. I'll yell when he brings out the horses and—"

The sleigh bells jangled wildly.

Tim shivered at the loud sound coming from the barn. Someone was shaking these bells too hard now! "Maybe Mr. Hanson can see me up here! Maybe he's trying to signal me! What if he's in trouble! Maybe he's been hurt!"

He glanced toward home. Georgie was outside waiting for the bus. But it wasn't in sight.

"If I go down to the barn, I'll miss the bus," he worried. "But if I don't—" He leaped down the slope. "Mom'll have to take me to school!"

He jumped up from a snowdrift and ran as fast as he could. The wild jangling of the sleigh bells frightened him. He wasn't sure he could do what might have to be done in that barn.

"If Mr. Hanson's hurt," he worried, "why doesn't Mrs. Hanson help him? Maybe she's in the basement and can't hear him. Or what if she's gone!" He might need Mrs. Hanson's help.

He raced past the farmhouse. The truck wasn't in the barnyard. "She *is* gone!" he gasped. "I'll have to do it by myself!" He tried to run faster toward the loud bells and the open barn door.

The bells were quiet now.

Then, a cow bawled.

"Aw, it's only a cow caught in the bell harness," he panted. But he kept running.

The cow bawled again.

Tim ran slower. "If both the Hansons are gone, I ran all the way to help a cow," he thought. "But maybe Mr. Hanson's hurt bad and can't shake the bells again!" He darted toward the wide doorway.

The barn was quiet. No bawling from the cow now. Not a tinkle from the bells.

"Mr. Hanson?" Tim called shakily from the doorway into the dark shadows. He stepped inside the barn. It was black, after the bright, white snow.

Thump. Thump. He knew it was a cow stomping somewhere, close. Close to the haymow. "If it's caught, why don't the bells jingle?" he wondered. "Mr. Hanson, are you all right?" He wished he could see better.

There was no answer.

"Mr. Hanson!" he shouted his loudest. He had to be sure it was only a cow in trouble.

"Yes, Tim."

Tim twisted around. Mr. Hanson was hurrying toward the barn! "Boy! Am I glad to see you!" cried Tim. "I thought you were hurt when the sleigh bells—"

The bells jangled wildly inside the barn.

Tim jumped outside. The sound was close. Too close! "See what I mean!" he gulped. "Something's in trouble. Must be a cow caught."

Mr. Hanson ran into the barn. "Keep out, Tim," he ordered. "Stay away from the door!"

Quickly Tim pushed his back against the outside of the barn. Then, slowly, he peeked around the doorway. Everything still looked black inside. But he could hear snorting and thumping and loud bells.

"Get back, Tim," said Mr. Hanson.

Tim jerked his head into the sunlight. Now he could hear Mr. Hanson talking softly, calmly to the snorting animal. But the snorting didn't sound like a cow. More like a horse. But how could a horse get caught in a bell harness? And if it did, why didn't it run out into the barnyard? He listened and waited. Mr. Hanson might need his help.

All at once a large animal leaped out of the barn!

Tim flattened himself against the barn. Then he gasped. It was the big buck. He was galloping across the snow!

"He's still wearing the bells!" Tim said aloud.

"I just hope he can't rub them off," Mr. Hanson said behind him. "I put them on him."

"But he was caught!" said Tim, puzzled.

"He was caught in the haymow rope, and I cut him loose," explained Mr. Hanson. "That old buck's been stealing too much hay from the barn, and frightening my cows. So, one day when I was feeding him some carrots—he's pretty tame with me, you know—I buckled on the bells."

"Now the hunters will know he's your pet!" added Tim with a teasing smile.

"Well," grinned Mr. Hanson. "I sort of thought of that, too, Tim. But come on, boy. You missed the bus, you know. I promised Georgie I'd find you and take you to school."

And then Tim remembered the hockey game and the Christmas trees. But he asked, "Was there any special reason for going over to our house this morning?"

"Well," said Mr. Hanson, "I tried to call you, Tim, but the line was busy. So I drove over to your place. Thought you might like to know we'd be needing you in the spruce woods tomorrow."

"Tomorrow!" sighed Tim. "Boy, that's swell!"

"I thought today was just right for a game of hockey," added Mr. Hanson.

And Tim agreed.

MYSTERY IN THE MOONLIT MEADOW

Mark blinked up at the full moon and turned over again in his sleeping bag. He wished he could go to sleep. All the other boys had been quiet for a long time. But he kept hearing strange sounds, sounds he had never heard at night in the city.

"Maybe I'll feel better when Mr. Passos walks around camp again," he hoped.

"Mark? Are you awake?" whispered Billy in the next sleeping bag.

"Yes!" Mark answered quickly and smiled over at Billy.

"I can't sleep, either," said Billy. "I keep thinking about all the things we'll start doing tomorrow. Last year was terrific here!"

"This is my first time to camp out," said Mark. "I've never even been in a woods before."

"It's only a little woods," Billy whispered excitedly, "but we sure have fun! Just wait'll we hike to. . . ."

Mark knew why Billy stopped talking. Soft music was coming from somewhere. Mark looked quickly at the other sleeping bags. "Maybe one of the boys is hiding a transistor radio," he said.

Billy's head was turning from side to side, listening. "No," he said. "I think it's coming from the meadow, beyond the woods."

"I didn't know campers were down there, too," said Mark.

"They aren't, but"—Billy was unzipping his sleeping bag—"Mr. Passos is, and with a radio, I'll bet. And he's probably shooting his silver arrows in the moonlight. You should've seen him last year.

He was terrific. He was a champion archer once in Greece." Billy pulled on jeans and a yellow shirt, and began putting on his shoes.

"I'd like to watch him, too," said Mark. He wiggled out of his warm bag. "Will Joe McWhirt mind?"

"The counselor? No," said Billy. "Joe knows I know the little woods pretty well. And the meadow's close to camp. And Mr. Passos is down there. Anyway, Joe's asleep."

Mark pulled on his shoes and jumped up, buttoning his shirt. He grinned at Billy. "Which way?"

"Just follow me," whispered Billy. "Keep close to my yellow shirt in the woods."

Mark followed him between the rows of sleeping boys. They passed the cook's tent and ran into the dark woods. Dry branches snapped. Leaves crunched as they trotted between trees. Patches of moonlight helped to light their way.

Mark kept his eyes on the yellow shirt and hoped he wouldn't stumble over some little animal.

"Music's getting louder," called Billy. "Bet Mr. Passos is waiting for the news to come on, just like my Dad does every night."

"Sure is strange music," panted Mark. "Sounds like . . . just a flute . . . or something. No horns, or anything." Suddenly his ears tingled. The music sighed loudly like the wind. Then it seemed to chirp and twitter like a bird. The eerie sounds made Mark shiver. He wasn't sure he liked being in the woods at night.

"Meadow's ahead!" called Billy. "Better stay behind the trees until we see which way he's shooting the arrows."

They crept to the edge of the woods and looked out into the bright moonlight. Something was in the middle of the meadow! It was white and flowing! Like a ghost!

"What's that?" Mark gulped and hid behind a tree.

"It could be some kind of new target," Billy answered calmly.

Mark peeked around the tree. "But where's Mr. Passos?"

"Look!" cried Billy. "It's moving!"

They watched the white, flowing thing sway and bend and jump in the moonlight.

"Billy," Mark whispered. "It's dancing to the flute music! Is it a ghost?"

"Whoever heard of a haunted meadow!" Billy said boldly. "But I still can't tell what it is."

Suddenly Mark felt he couldn't breathe! The ghost-thing was running toward the trees. Toward *them!* He hugged the tree and closed his eyes. "Don't let it see you, Billy," he begged.

All at once Billy was pressing against Mark's back. "Maybe we can tell what it is, if it passes us," he whispered. Now, he sounded frightened.

They waited for sounds of something rushing past them into the woods. But only the flute twittered softly somewhere.

Then, Mark felt Billy move away from him and the tree. "I'll take another quick look," said Billy.

Slowly Mark leaned out and looked, too. The ghost-thing was dancing away from the woods. "Could it be one of those forest fairies in stories?" he asked shyly.

"If it is"—Billy turned to Mark and grinned—"then I'm a giant elf! Don't be afraid. It's either a real person dancing, or something Mr. Passos is working on. He really scares us on ghost-story night."

"Sure!" hoped Mark. "And it's on thin wires hooked to trees!"

"And here his ghost comes again!" laughed Billy.

Mark took only a quick look at the running thing in the meadow. And he closed his eyes. It was still too spooky for him. And maybe it wasn't a trick Mr. Passos was working on. And who would be dancing in the meadow at night? And where was the flute music coming from?

"It's coming closer this time!" cried Billy.

Quickly Mark turned away from the meadow. "What if it is a real ghost, Billy! Come on!" He ran, fast, into the darkness.

But Billy's yellow shirt didn't flash past him. And Mark was too frightened to stop running. He darted from one patch of moonlight to another.

Suddenly a black log was ahead of him. He slid to a stop. "We didn't come this way!" he worried. Around and around he turned. Nothing looked familiar. He couldn't hear Billy walking through the leaves. But the flute was still playing. He just hoped the ghost was still in the meadow!

"Billy!" Mark cried wildly. "I'm lost!"

"Over here!" answered Billy from nearby.

Mark turned around again. He could find no yellow shirt. "Where are you?" he yelled.

"Over here. To your right!" answered Billy.

Mark ran as fast as he could to the right. And there in the moonlight was Billy's yellow shirt.

"You were just a few trees away from camp," said Billy. "Hope we didn't wake up everybody. They'll think we're lost in here."

"I was!" shivered Mark. He followed the yellow shirt out of the woods.

The camp was quiet. No one was up. Silently they walked toward the cook's tent.

Just then from the shadows among the tents the white, flowing ghost-thing appeared!

Mark couldn't take another step. Billy didn't move, either. But the ghost-thing kept coming closer!

"Boys?" it spoke softly. "I was coming to find you." It sounded like a woman. And it was walking, not flowing. And there was no flute music.

"What do you want?" Billy asked bravely.

Now it was close enough for Mark to see dark eyes

that sparkled in the moonlight.

It smiled and said, "I'm Mrs. Passos and—"

"I sure am glad!" cried Mark.

"And *you* were in the meadow!" laughed Billy.

"Yes," said Mrs. Passos. "I was dancing."

"But where was that funny music coming from?" Mark asked quickly.

"That was Mr. Passos playing the shepherd's pipe in the tree shadows," she explained. "It's supposed to sound like the night wind and night birds. We were practicing for tomorrow night's program," she added.

"For us?" frowned Billy.

"No, for my girls," smiled Mrs. Passos. "Our camp's down the road. And every year when the moon is full, I dance a very old Grecian dance of a wood nymph. Sort of a Greek fairy that dances in the moonlight. My girl campers love it."

"We never had girls around last year," said Billy.

"Oh, we were in your meadow then," laughed Mrs. Passos. "Remember the night Joe McWhirt took you boys on a moonlight hike?"

"Sure!" said Billy. "We have one tomorrow—"

"Boys!" Someone was shouting in the woods.

"That's Mr. Passos," she explained. "He thinks you're still lost. Better get back into your bags. I'll go find him!"

Mark didn't wait for Billy to lead the way. He ran to his sleeping bag and scooted into it. When he closed his eyes, he could see a dancing ghost in the moonlit meadow. "That'll be a swell story to tell on ghost-story night!" he thought happily. And soon he was asleep.

THE SHORTCUT HOME

"No cars coming! Let's go!" said Tom. He held Andy's hand as they ran across the wide highway. They stopped running and started walking at the edge of Snyder's Woods.

"Here's the shortcut," said Tom. He followed the path through the trees.

"We didn't play so long at Scotty's . . . that we

can't look . . . in the hawk's nest, did we?" panted Andy behind Tom.

"We have time," Tom told him. "But maybe she hasn't laid eggs yet this spring." A few steps later he walked away from the path. "Over this way."

"I remember," said Andy. "And there's the same old log!"

They jumped over the log and trotted toward a long row of thick bushes.

"Be careful of the thorny branches," warned Tom. "They've grown a lot since last fall."

"I remember them, too," Andy answered.

Carefully they pushed their way through thick, thorny, leafy bushes.

"Something sure smells smoky in here," said Tom.

"Bet Mr. Snyder's burning old logs," said Andy. "Wish we had some hot dogs!"

Tom held up the last thorny branches for Andy to pass under. "I'll climb up and look in the nest so we can hurry," said Tom. He turned around, expecting to see the tall elm he was going to climb. "It's gone!" he gulped.

"Lots of trees are gone!" cried Andy.

They stared, puzzled, at a long wide field where once a thick woods had been. Wide circles of black ashes and small hills of sand dotted the burned grass all around them.

"Wonder what Mr. Snyder's going to do back here?" Tom asked thoughtfully.

"Build a cabin, just for us!" joked Andy. He ran to a pile of sand.

"Maybe it's a—a—a flying saucer landing field!" teased Tom. "And their atomic energy's burned everything! Come on. We won't find the hawk's nest now." He watched as Andy started to slide down the sand.

"Tom!" yelled Andy. He was teetering halfway down the sand. "I found one!"

Tom trotted toward him. He expected to see a snake or maybe a broken hawk's egg. But on the other side of the sand hill was a big, shiny, round thing.

"Yowee!" cried Tom.

"It's bigger than our kitchen table!" gulped Andy.

"And almost as tall!" added Tom. He moved closer and tapped the big round thing. "Looks like the metal on car bumpers. But it doesn't sound like metal."

Andy scooted down the hill. "Boy! It sure looks like flying saucers look!" he smiled up at Tom.

"Sure, Andy. Lots of them landed here!" teased Tom.

"Aw," sighed Andy. "It's just some machine Mr. Snyder's using." He crawled around the rim of the round thing.

"See anything?" Tom asked quickly when Andy's head disappeared.

"A window!" cried Andy. He jumped up and backed away from the round thing. "And there's a little door, Tom! I couldn't see in, but—"

Tom scrambled out of the sand. "Let's get out of here! It couldn't be a real saucer. But if it is, I don't want to see any little people coming out of it!"

"Maybe they're already out of it!" gulped Andy.

Tom glanced quickly around the burned field. No one was watching them—unless someone was in the shadows of the trees. And trees were all around the field!

"Hurry back to the shortcut!" Tom told Andy.

"It's the quickest way home!" He ran toward the bushes. Andy raced after him.

They moved as fast as they could through the thorny branches. Suddenly Tom heard voices beyond the bushes. He turned back and pushed down on Andy's head.

Andy sat down quickly. "What's the matter?" he whispered.

"Voices," whispered Tom. He pointed ahead and crouched under the branches near Andy.

"The Martians are coming back!" Andy cried softly.

Tom could hear no words, just mumbling. He tried to see who was talking. The bushes were too thick.

"What if they have extra strong eyes! And ears!" worried Andy. "And a ray gun!"

Tom didn't answer. He hoped *they* wouldn't come into the bushes. And he watched the ground ahead for feet—big feet, or little feet!

"Tom!" whispered Andy. "They sound like real people now. Maybe the Martians changed themselves to look like we do."

Tom didn't answer. He was beginning to hear words now, words like *martian* and *planet* and *saucer.*

"We've got to get out of here fast!" Tom whispered to Andy. "Without them seeing us. I think they're sitting on that old log near the shortcut. You go first, back through the bushes. Run fast across the field into the woods. We'll try to find the shortcut over there!"

Slowly, quietly they turned around under the thorny branches.

All at once the voices were louder. Quickly Tom looked back. No little people were under the branches. Not yet. He grabbed Andy's shirt to keep him from crawling out of the bushes. And they became as still as two rocks. Now they could hear everything the voices said.

"How many can we take at one time in the big saucer?" asked a man on the other side of the bushes.

"About a hundred and twenty," answered another man.

"Better get the heavy equipment down here to finish this job," said the first man.

"It's due down, tomorrow," answered the other man.

Just then Tom felt Andy nudging him. "Let's go ho—"

Tom pressed his hand against Andy's mouth.

The men's voices were quiet.

"They heard, Andy!" Tom worried. "They'll find us!"

Then, "Are you sure it will all be finished before summer?" asked a man's voice.

"It has to be, if we want this saucer landing—"

Suddenly Tom heard rustling behind him. He

turned and saw Andy crawling fast under the branches. Tom knew he had to follow him. The end of the bushes was near. Maybe they could make it to the woods. The men were still talking, but he couldn't listen now. He hurried after Andy.

At the edge of the field, they darted out of the bushes.

"Stop!" shouted a man.

Tom and Andy kept running toward the woods.

"Where are they?" asked Andy.

"I don't know!" said Tom. "Don't look back!"

"Hope they don't have ray guns!" gasped Andy.

They were almost to the trees when, "Wait!" the man shouted again.

Tom shoved Andy into the woods. "Run home!" he cried. But Andy fell to the ground. Tom pulled him up. "Go on! I'll try to make them chase me."

"Look!" gasped Andy.

Tom twisted around. Two men, two real-looking men, were pushing their way through the bushes.

"Wait a minute, boys," shouted one of the men.

Tom and Andy stood still, staring at the men. "They're just men, I think," Tom said quietly.

"I sure hope so!" said Andy.

"Let's see what they want," Tom told him.

They watched the two men hurry out of the bushes. "You boys will have to stay out of this area," called a man. "We'll be cutting out more trees and burning stumps before building the big saucer."

"That's why everything's so burned!" Andy whispered excitedly. "But why are they going to build a big saucer here?"

"Maybe it's some kind of secret scientific experiment," Tom answered. "We'll soon find out!"

The men hurried across the burned grass. "You boys didn't move our plastic model over there, did you?" one of the men asked. He nodded toward the big, shiny round thing.

Tom and Andy smiled happily at each other. "No, sir. We didn't!" answered Tom.

"We're just taking the shortcut home!" added Andy.

"Well," smiled the man, "better not come this way for a few weeks. Our heavy equipment is due here to build the roadway and cement parking space."

"Is it a secret experiment?" asked Tom.

The man laughed. "I hope not! We want everybody to *know* we'll be serving the best Martian Malts, and Planet Potatoes, and Saucer Sandwiches in town. Right here at the Saucer Landing Drive-In Restaurant. It'll be ready before summer."

"Oh, boy!" laughed Andy. "A flying saucer for real people!"

"We'll be seeing you then!" Tom smiled at the man. "Come on, Andy." And Tom led the way through the woods to the shortcut home.

A NIGHT IN THE ATTIC

Pete had forgotten he had so many cousins. And aunts. And uncles. Today Grandmother and Grandfather's old farmhouse was filled with them. And tomorrow everyone would celebrate Grandmother and Grandfather's wedding anniversary. But tonight—

"We have a problem," said Grandfather. "We're almost out of beds. Some of the boys will have to sleep in the attic. Unless one of you wants Old Sandy's rug in the kitchen." He winked at Pete. Then at Johnny. "All right with you, boys?"

Pete said "Sure!" So did Johnny.

"There are *three* cots up there," said Grandfather, smiling.

"I want to sleep in the attic," cried Joey, Pete's little brother.

"Good boys. Now hurry up to bed," said Grandfather. "Pete will show you the way. Old Sandy and I have to check the chickens."

Quickly the three boys changed into their pajamas, then rushed to the attic door. It squeaked loudly as Pete opened it. A dim light bulb glowed at the top of the steep stairs. Pete started up first. Then Joey. The steps creaked under their sock-covered feet.

Johnny's untied shoes clopped noisily behind them. "I've never been up here," he said excitedly.

"I won't come alone," said Joey. "It's too dark and spooky!"

"Oh, it's just like any other old attic. Filled with junk," Pete told them.

At the top of the stairs they saw the three cots in a row.

Joey jumped into the middle one. "I'm here!"

"I'll take the one near the stairs," said Johnny. He was looking around at dusty furniture, stacks of boxes, and old clothes hanging on a high wire. "Just in case we need a drink or something," he added. He stepped out of his shoes and stretched out on his cot.

Pete reached up to turn off the light. "Okay, fellas?"

"You know I always have a little light," said Joey.

"And we could talk awhile," added Johnny hopefully.

"Okay," agreed Pete. "But I better close the door so the little kids won't climb up here." He hurried down the creaky steps and closed the squeaky door. When he got back to his cot, he scooted under the cool sheet and listened to the trees rustling above the roof.

"Sure is nice and peaceful up here," Johnny said sleepily.

"And not very spooky," added Joey.

RORRRK! RORRRK!

"What was that, Pete?" Joey sat up quickly.

So did Johnny.

RORRRK! RORRRK!

"It's up there near the roof," cried Johnny.

"Aw"—Pete smiled over at them—"haven't you ever heard tree limbs rubbing each other? It's windy outside."

"Well, it sure sounded like some wild animal," Johnny replied uneasily.

"Yessirree!" agreed Joey.

"Not if you know what caused it," Pete explained and yawned.

RORRRK! RORRK!

"Ugh. I can't go to sleep with that rorrrking," complained Joey.

"Aw, count your dinosaurs," teased Pete.

"They're too monster-y. I'll count Grandfather's chickens," Joey giggled, and began counting quietly.

Pete was tired and ready for sleep. He turned away from the light bulb. A spotted face was only inches away from him. In a flash he was wide awake! So was the spotted face. He blinked at it.

Then he realized he was looking into a dusty, spotted mirror leaning against a box. All the same, he turned back toward the light.

Joey was already asleep. Johnny was looking around at the attic junk. Pete closed his eyes, hoping he could feel sleepy again. He wished that spotted mirror hadn't been there.

"Pete," Johnny whispered. "What's th-th-that?"

"Where?" Pete sat up quickly.

Johnny pointed to the dark rafter above Pete's cot.

Two shiny, greenish eyes were watching them.

"It's a squirrel, I think," Pete told him. "Don't wake up Joey."

"Will it attack us?" worried Johnny.

Pete shook his head and moved to get a better look at the green eyes. They were gone! But a soft clickety-clickety sound ran down the rafter.

"What if it comes back, Pete?" asked Johnny.

"I was just thinking about that," answered Pete. He got up and pulled his cot from under the rafter. "Just in case it jumps down," he explained. And he backed into the old clothes hanging on the high

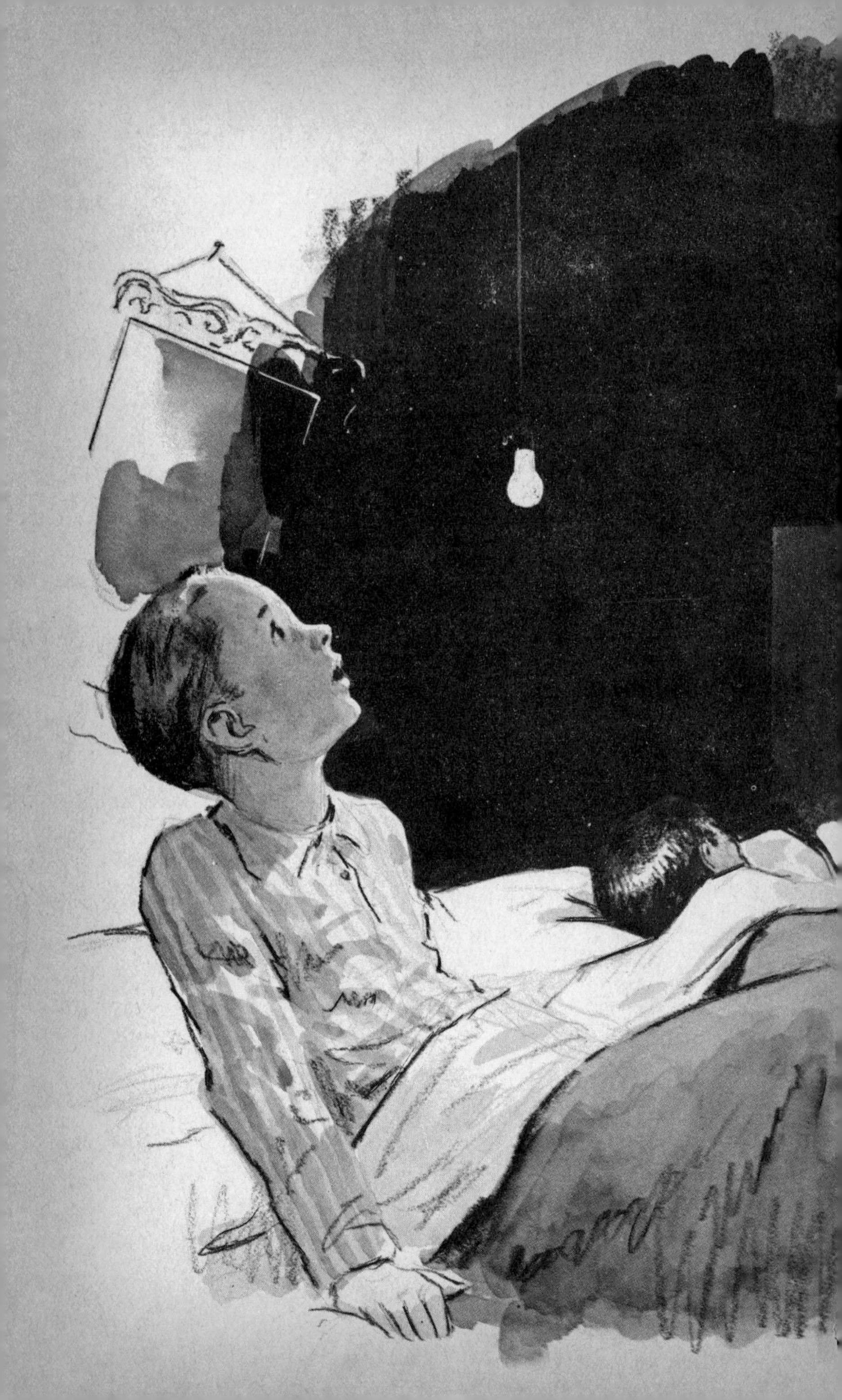

wire. Something screeched behind him! He dropped to his cot and turned around.

A squirrel was crawling over the shoulders of an old suit!

"There it goes," cried Johnny. "Under the furniture!"

"Boy!" Pete said after a deep breath. "I hope that's the last one!"

"Couldn't we find room for the cots downstairs?" Johnny asked hopefully.

"But we'd have to wake up Joey," Pete reasoned. "And squirrels won't hurt us." But Pete watched the old suit. Maybe there was another squirrel in it. Maybe it would jump on his cot, or Joey's. And he wasn't sure a squirrel wouldn't bite.

Suddenly the sleeve of the old suit fluttered.

"Pete!" called Johnny. "That suit—"

"I saw it," Pete whispered. "Maybe it's a baby squirrel." He watched a little lump in the sleeve.

"Two of them!" Johnny cried softly.

Pete saw a little lump wiggle in the other sleeve.

All at once the suit moved on the wire! Slowly it slid toward them.

Pete jerked a sheet over Joey's head. "They might jump down on Joey," he whispered.

"Hit it!" begged Johnny. "Maybe they'll fall out and run. Here!" He tossed his shoe onto Pete's cot.

Pete grabbed it and threw hard. The shoe hit the pants. The suit danced on the wire a few seconds. Then it only swayed. But the two lumps stayed in the sleeves. And one lump was wiggling down, down, until . . . a tiny face peeked out at them.

"A mouse!" sighed Johnny.

Pete gulped. Behind the face wiggled a black, winged body with claws clutching the edge of the sleeve!

"Bats!" shrieked Johnny. He rolled under his cot.

Pete knew something had to be done before the bats got loose in the attic. Slowly he reached out and gently rippled a pants leg. He hoped this time the bat would wiggle back into the sleeve. It did! "Open the window, Johnny!" he said. "And make it fast!"

Johnny stood up stiffly. "What window?"

Pete nodded toward the end of the attic behind the suit.

Johnny inched his way past the suit, then rushed to the window.

Carefully Pete lifted the suit hanger from the wire. He walked slowly toward the end of the attic. And he watched the sleeves. The lumps were quiet.

"I can't—push—it—open!" grunted Johnny.

"Pull it!" urged Pete. He was almost to the window. The lumps were wiggling down, down again!

BANG! The window opened! A breeze rushed in. The suit danced.

Quickly Pete pushed the suit out the window. A strong breeze whipped it off the hanger. And, in the moonlight, he watched the old suit drift down onto a tree limb. "No more bats *or* old suit to worry about now." He smiled at Johnny and closed the window. "But we'll have to climb a tree tomorrow!"

"Boy," sighed Johnny. "I could sleep for a week."

They crawled wearily back into their cots. Pete even smiled into the spotted mirror. He was too tired to worry about anything in the attic now. He knew Johnny was, too.

They were almost asleep, when—

SQUEEEAK!

"Johnny?" Pete whispered sleepily.

"I heard it. I'm not afraid now," mumbled Johnny.

But Pete listened. The squeak was too loud for a mouse. He glanced up at the rafters. No squirrels in sight. The old clothes weren't moving again.

Thump. Thump. Clack-clack. Creeeak!

That noise was on the stairs! Pete and Johnny sat up at the same time. Their eyes were glued to the top step.

Thump. Thump. Clack-clack. Creeeak!

"Pete?" called a soft voice. And Grandfather's head popped above the top step. Then Old Sandy clack-clacked up the rest of the steps, padded over to Johnny, and pushed his nose into his hand.

"I brought up Old Sandy for company," smiled Grandfather. "Just in case we didn't chase out all the pesky little squirrels before you came. They get in once in a while. But they stay away from Old Sandy."

"Thanks, Grandfather," smiled Pete.

"We're not afraid," added Johnny.

"Now, get some sleep. No more ghost-story-telling." Grandfather winked. "You stay here, Sandy. Good night, boys."

"Night," answered Pete and Johnny.

Old Sandy flopped down beside Johnny's cot.

Grandfather thumped down the creaky stairs.

After the attic door squeaked closed, Johnny whispered, "Sure is exciting, sleeping in the attic. But I'm glad we're going home tomorrow night."

"Me, too," Pete mumbled sleepily.

And they fell asleep in the attic.

THE TOWER

Diane flopped down in the cool leafy dirt. "I don't care if they do catch up with us, Peg. I'm hot and tired."

"But the tower's a *good* place to hide!" Peg called down the tree-covered hill. "And I want to see the river before Mrs. Cummings rings the lunch bell. Come on, Di. Please?"

Diane got up slowly. To please her friend she started up the hill again. "We're pretty far away from the class's shelter house."

"Well—" Panting, Peg was waiting for her. "They won't find us. Unless they know how to get to my tower, too."

"You and your tower," sighed Diane. But soon she was close behind Peg.

"I've wanted to climb up to it for a long time, Di. But we always go to the other end of the park," said Peg.

"Too many school picnics in McGrew Park today. Guess that's why we got this end. But I never heard Brian or anyone else talk about your old tower."

"Good." Peg was over the top of the hill. "Hurry! It's beautiful up here."

A few more grunts and Diane was beside her. They were standing near a tall stone tower in a small meadow.

"There's the top of our shelter house," said Diane.

But Peg was looking across the winding river far below them. "Oh, look! Such beautiful hills over there."

"Peg! The tower's on a lookout point. Right on the edge of a cliff." Diane moved backwards.

Peg crept closer to the edge. "Gee, wonder why there's no guardrail?"

"Are you sure this is in McGrew Park?" Diane's eyes followed the hilltop. The small meadow ran into a clump of trees. Two sides ended with steep, wooded hills. And there was the cliff.

"I guess so," Peg answered matter-of-factly. "Let's go into the tower, before Brian and the others catch up with us." She led the way around the side of the building to a dark wooden door.

"I kind of hope it's locked, Peg. Maybe we should go back," Diane worried. "We could find a closer hiding place."

Peg shook her head. She pulled a saucer-sized shiny brass ring. And the heavy door opened slowly. Bright sunlight reflected on a spotless, white marble floor. A polished brass handrail glistened above fancy black iron steps.

"Oh, isn't it elegant," gulped Peg. "And a winding stairway! Wonder how many steps there are to the top?"

She began to climb, counting excitedly. In a few seconds she had disappeared around the first turn of the almost dark stairway. Her footsteps echoed eerily.

Diane felt uneasy about this unusual tower. No one but Peg seemed to know about it. But she pulled herself upward and around the cool stone wall. The sunlight below was fading with each step. She didn't welcome the black steps ahead, the ones she wouldn't be able to see. She listened to Peg's cheerful count-

ing and began to feel a little bolder.

"Forty-four, forty-five. It's getting lighter. I'm near the top!"

Carefully, Diane began taking two steps at a time. Her footsteps *clinked,* then echoed in the darkness.

"I'm at the top! Fifty-four steps! Oh, it's glorious," called Peg.

A few moments later, Diane was very glad to join her at the top of the tower.

"Watch the hilltop for the others, Di." Peg pointed to a wide, open window. "I want to study the river from this window."

Diane found the hilltop they had just climbed. She gazed out into the sunlight, then listened to the soft breeze. "I hear lots of yelling. But none's near enough to tell Brian's voice." She leaned against the warm stones. "I feel like a light in a lighthouse."

"I saw flashes! Across the river!" Peg cried.

"Just a reflection," Diane said lazily.

Peg was quiet for a while. But then she almost shouted, "It's a message, Di! I know! Remember my telegraph set, for Christmas? Blink . . . blink —I'm sure it's Morse code!" She mumbled to herself.

"Well, what's the message, chief?" Diane teased.

"They keep repeating it. Whatever could P—KB4 mean, Di?"

Diane, still watching the hilltop, was ready to answer with something silly. But she heard a soft echo rising up the dark stairway. "Peg, somebody's down there. I heard the door close. And no one came up the hill. Honest."

Peg stared anxiously at her. They listened hard to hear the next noise.

"Brian's smart enough to find a different way up that hill if he thought we'd be able to see him from up here," Peg whispered.

Diane agreed with a nod. "But I wish we could hide and scare them."

Peg moved quickly to the thick stone post in the center of the tower. She pointed to a small door above the floor. "It's a cupboard, I think." And she opened the door.

Diane peeked in first. "It's not even dirty. But there's something in here. Looks sort of like a lamp."

"It's a blinker light, Di! To send messages with! Gee, maybe we found a nest of spies!"

Diane turned toward the dark stairway. "Sshh. They're coming up." She crawled into a corner of the cupboard. Peg squeezed in between her and the lamp.

Footsteps *clinked* slowly upward.

"Di"—Peg pressed against her—"it doesn't really sound like Brian or—"

"They're just trying to scare us. You know Brian. If he can find the tower, he can think up something scary."

But Diane felt sure such heavy footsteps weren't Brian's. And she hoped it wasn't someone they wouldn't want to meet. *Maybe,* she thought, *he's coming to chase us out of the tower.*

Clink, clink echoed the metal stairs.

"I wish one of the kids would giggle or something," Peg said with a shiver.

"Sshh." Diane crossed all her fingers. She wished hard for it to be Brian.

"What if it's a spy coming to send more secret messages," worried Peg. "He'll have to get this lamp and—"

"Be quiet, Peg!" Diane wished Peg didn't have such a good imagination. Now, she was beginning to believe in real spies.

CLINK. CLINK. CLINK. Then, all was quiet. Now heavy, slow footsteps—not like Brian's—approached and stopped near the cupboard door.

Diane and Peg waited, hoping the noise would move farther away from them.

But the next sound was a loud cough, not the cough of a child. And then the door opened. A large hand reached toward them. It touched Peg. She winced as it rubbed her knee. Quickly Diane tilted the lamp toward the hand. The hand grabbed it and pulled it out of the cupboard.

Diane had almost finished a silent sigh of relief when a face looked in at them!

At first the face looked unreal. It was long and thin with deep, shadowed wrinkles. And it was topped with chalk-white hair. But then the strange face smiled.

"Well, well. What have we here?" It was a friendly voice. "Come out, little squirrels. I'll not eat you."

Peg crawled out with a cheerful "Hello!" Diane followed her quietly. And they both looked up at a tall, white-haired old man, still smiling down at them.

"Where did you come from?" he asked pleasantly.

Peg pointed toward the park. "A picnic."

"A school picnic, I imagine." The old man looked out of the window facing the river. "Oh, my. I must take down this message." He fumbled in a pocket and found a pen and paper. "You go ahead and enjoy the view."

Diane whispered close to Peg's ear, "He doesn't look like a spy. But we'd better go, just in case."

But Peg only smiled and walked to the old man's side. "What are you doing?" she asked calmly.

The man kept writing and staring at the flashing light across the river.

Suddenly Diane darted to the window overlooking the hilltop. "They've found the tower! I hear Brian coming this way!"

"No! They mustn't!" The old man was frowning.

"But they're just trying to find us," she explained uneasily.

"They mustn't come here," he repeated louder.

Diane grabbed Peg's hand. "We'd better go."

"This tower is not in the park."

Peg looked surprised. "It isn't?"

"No." And then the old man smiled again and spoke gently. "This tower is in too dangerous a spot for children to play. I never meant for it to be part of the park. I'll have to put a fence along the hilltop, I guess." He sighed. "After all these years I

wouldn't want to lose my tower."

"It's my fault," Peg apologized. "I saw the tower from far away and always wanted to come here."

"Now that you understand, I hope you won't come back. Unless you come first to visit me and my wife, over beyond the meadow and that clump of trees. I'll be happy to share our wonderful view with you."

He gazed out of a window, then said thoughtfully, "You see, it's a very special place for me. An old, old friend and I signal each other every day. That's the way we play chess, by secret messages across the river," he added with a wink.

Peg looked thoughtful. "What does P—KB4 mean?"

The old man answered simply, "Pawn moves to king's bishop's fourth file."

So that was it! Diane breathed a relieved sigh. "Come on, Peg. We'll let them find us *in* the park!"

"Thank you, Mr.—?" Peg turned back to him.

"Mr. McGrew, just like the park," he answered with a smile. "Now, do come visit us."

"Thank you!" Peg started down the fifty-four winding steps. And Diane hurried behind her.

OPEN THE DOOR!

"I'm done," said Ray. He closed his notebook with a slap.

His sister Becky didn't look up from her book.

"Want some cocoa and crackers?" Ray asked. "Grandma fixed some before she went upstairs." He got up from the dining room table and headed for the kitchen stove. The clock behind the pan of cocoa showed eight fifteen.

"Mom and Dad are late," he called to Becky.

He was pouring cocoa into two cups when he heard a noise outside the house. "Here they are!" he yelled.

He hurried to the back door and flipped the outside light switch. He grabbed the doorknob, ready to let them in out of the cold, snowy winter night.

And he waited. But there was no other sound outside the door, only the wind and icy snow blowing against the windows.

"Where?" asked Becky, coming into the kitchen.

Ray shrugged his shoulders. "Just the wind, I guess, Beck. But I thought I heard them."

"Oh, you're too anxious for 'Pumfrey's, the Best by Taste Test, Potato Chips!' " teased Becky. And she went back to the dining room table.

Ray finished pouring the cocoa. He was reaching for the box of crackers when—

"Ray," Becky called to him. "Somebody's at the front door. You get it. I think Grandma's still in the bathtub."

Ray hurried through the dining room and into the living room. "I don't hear anything," he said in front of the door.

"Open it! I did hear someone out there," said Becky. "Maybe it's a neighbor, freezing."

Ray turned on the porch light. He peeked through the thin curtain covering the door window. "Uh, well, I don't see anyone," he said. "It was just the wind again."

"Well, it sounded like something was out there," Becky argued from the dining room.

"It had to be the wind," Ray said patiently. "The door rattled, that's all." He went back into the kitchen for his cocoa.

When he turned away from the stove, there was Becky behind him. And she looked frightened.

"Ray," she whispered, "it really didn't sound like the door rattling. It was sort of a thumping, and then a scratching." She hugged her arms and shivered. "Maybe we ought to see if Grandma's finished her bath and—"

THUMP! THUMP!

Ray and Becky, suddenly white-faced with fear, stared at the kitchen door.

"See? It doesn't sound like the wind," said Becky. "And I'm afraid."

Ray pushed down hard on the top of his tingling head. His heart pounded as he tried to speak calmly. "Uh, it's probably Mom and Dad this time." He took a step toward the door.

THUMP! THUMP!

Becky grabbed his arm. "What if it isn't Mom and Dad?"

"Well," Ray took a deep breath for courage, "I'll just open the door and see. What's there to be afraid of?"

He hoped he sounded braver than he felt. Stiffly he reached for the doorknob.

THUMP! THUMP! THUMP! This time it was even louder.

Ray jerked his hand back.

"Go get Grandma!" begged Becky.

Ray stepped back from the door. "Dad? Mom?" he called.

There was no answer. Not even a *thump*.

"See? No one." He spoke a little more calmly. "It's just a broken branch, or something near the door banging in the wind. I'll open the door and prove it. You'll see."

The doorknob felt cold in his hand, and he turned it slowly.

"Don't open it, please, Ray," cried Becky. "Just peek out."

Ray was glad to let go of that knob. Quickly he pulled the Venetian blind cord and looked between the slats.

"What's there?" Becky tugged at his arm.

"I can't see anything," he told her. "The window's all covered with ice and snow on the outside."

"Maybe it *is* just the wind and a branch from the old apple tree," Becky hoped.

"Sure it is, Beck," Ray answered with an understanding smile. "Let's have some cocoa." His heart was still pounding too hard, but he felt less afraid now. He knew Grandma would be downstairs soon. "Let's see what's on TV."

"That's a wonderful idea," sighed Becky.

They carried their cups and crackers to the living room. Becky curled up on the sofa. But before Ray could turn on the television set—

THUMP! SCRATCH-SCRATCH!

"Ooooh!" cried Becky. "I want Grandma!"

TV
PROGRAM

Ray knew *that* wasn't another broken branch outside the front door! He didn't move. "Sshh," he whispered to Becky.

They listened to the thumping and scratching. And it didn't stop this time.

Becky began to cry softly. "Ray, please, go get Grandma. I'm so afraid, with the front door and the back door—"

"Just a minute," he whispered. He couldn't tell her the fearful thoughts flashing through his head. *What'll I do now? What if it's something I wouldn't want to see? Why doesn't Grandma hurry?*

He took a deep breath and spoke softly. "Listen. It's stopped. Maybe it's gone now. And I can't tell Grandma. If she's still in the tub and I tell her someone's at the door, she'll tell me to open it and—"

The thumping, scratching began again. It was much louder. Even the wind seemed to howl across the porch.

Ray watched Becky hide her head under a pillow.

And then, "See who's at the door, Ray," Grandma called. "I'll be down in just a minute."

Ray stiffened his shoulders. He swallowed hard. "Yes, Grandma."

"I'm not going to look," Becky mumbled from under the pillow. But Ray could see her eyes watching him.

"Hurry, Ray." It was Grandma's voice again.

Ray couldn't hurry to that door even though he did feel braver. He didn't look through the thin curtain. A peek at who or what it was out there didn't matter now. He twisted the icy knob.

The door opened, and he stared straight ahead into the wintery night. The dim porch light showed no one, nothing.

All at once he felt almost calm and slightly silly at being so frightened. He put one foot onto the slippery porch for a look to be sure everything was really all right.

BANG! The front door hit the inside wall! Shivers ran down Ray's back, but quickly he remembered the strong, gusty wind.

"Ray!" His grandmother was at the top of the stairs. "Close the door, quickly."

He stepped back into the living room. But before

he could close the door, something bumped his leg! Then a cold, wet thing touched his hand once, twice. He closed his eyes tightly, afraid to look.

Becky squealed! The lampshade jiggled.

"Ray!" Becky cried loudly.

He opened his eyes and saw Becky catching the lampshade. And there beside her was a small, friendly-looking Dachshund sniffing her shoes.

"A little dog!" said Becky, almost in tears, but smiling. "He ran in when the door was open."

"I should've looked down, too," said Ray with a grin. And he closed the front door. "It was only a little dog at the door, Grandma," he called up the stairway. He watched the little dog wagging its long tail as it wiggled its way toward the kitchen.

"Oh, the poor thing. Out on a night like this," called Grandma. "Give it something to eat. I'll go ahead and straighten the bathroom."

Ray raced after Becky to the kitchen. "I'll get some bread. You get milk. Wonder where he lives?"

"I don't care!" said Becky happily. "I'm just glad it was only a little dog trying to get in. Weren't we kind of silly to be afraid?"

Ray didn't have time to answer. There was a sudden loud pounding at the back door!

"Oh, no!" squealed Becky. "What was that?" She ran into the dining room.

"It can't be another dog," Ray told himself. But he called to Becky, "Don't be afraid, Beck. Remember the branch from the old apple tree and that strong wind?" He hoped that was all it was at the back door.

The little dog began growling and sniffing at the bottom of the door.

"Let Grandma open it this time," Becky called from the other room.

But Ray moved closer to the dog and the door.

BANG! BANG! BANG!

"Ray! Open the door! We're freezing out here! And get this big branch out of the doorway!"

Ray felt like sinking to the floor. "Mom and Dad are home!" he yelled to Becky.

Gladly he opened the door.

THE AUTHOR

It all began back in Crawfordsville, Indiana, where Mildred Bingham grew up, the oldest of five children. Her goal at the age of ten was to someday write for children. This led her to journalism studies at Indiana University, and on to a newspaper column, plays for educational radio, work as an editor for several radio stations, and work as a publicist. But finally she got around to fulfilling that promise she made to herself as a child: writing for children. She has been unusually successful, with stories appearing in a number of children's magazines and in collections of stories.

Mrs. Bingham makes her home in Dayton, Ohio, and has many interests in addition to her writing. Chief among these are son Tim, a bright, happy six-year-old, and husband Theodore, a newspaper editor. She also finds time to work as a group leader of a church-sponsored national study of children in church schools, and to enjoy children, dogs, flowers, and sewing.

An active life, with lots of interests, has led to the many stories gathered together in IT'S A MYSTERY!